BoJo's W...

Crapping on Britain since August 2019

Catastrophus

Editorial

In the autumn of 2019, an incompetent narcissist called a general election, which he inexplicably went on to win. Future historians will no doubt spend years trying to work out how and why he managed it.

This book will not help them.

It documents key moments of full-on awfulness during the election campaign, and the weeks that followed, right up to the ultimate self-destructive act of Brexit Day.

Throughout this period, Johnson and his Tories showed us exactly who they were, but the electorate* chose not to listen.

*Well, 44% of them. Britain has a really stupid electoral system

We could cry. But laughing is better. Britain's worst ever Prime Minister is also its most ridiculous, and hopefully this book will make you feel a little bit better about the awful state of our country.

Enjoy!

Dr Richard Milne.

SOLD

PROPERTY OF D. TRUMP

BoJo's Woe Show

Editions **1-52**

Crapping on Britain
since August 2019

Catastrophus *Copulatus*

Book 1: November 2019
to February 2020

We nicked this idea from Labour.

DEDICATION:

This book would not exist without the extraordinary malice and incompetence of Boris Johnson, the Tories, and everyone else who inflicted Brexit upon the UK. I therefore dedicate this book to anyone and everyone who has stood against them, in any way, since 2016. It is always better to fight for what is good and what is right, whether you win or lose.

Thanks are due to Andrew Milne for certain background images, my wife for love and patience, and everyone on Twitter who has supported me and retweeted my Woe Show cartoons, and hence made me feel that doing this book would be worthwhile.

ABOUT THE AUTHOR:

Dr Richard Milne is a scientist with a healthy obsession about plants, and a passion for critical thinking. He began drawing cartoons while at school, and very occasionally these were read by someone other than his brother. He was as surprised as anyone when, decades later, he started drawing them again on Twitter in response to the insanity of Brexit. He somehow fits them in between teaching, hunting plants, writing scientific papers, fatherhood, eating, sleeping, cooking and washing up.

This is his first cartoon anthology book, but more will follow, plus a first novel, *Misjudgement Day*.

According to one commentator on Twitter, Dr Milne is better looking than the selfie cartoon here.
However. that is probably just a reflection on his limited art skills.

BoJo's Woe Show

Edition 1

Crapping on Britain since August 2019

Catastrophus *Copulatus*

8th November 2019

Election called for December 12th

Grenfell victims "lacked common sense" says Jacob Rees Mogg

Phwoffle. Phwiffle phwaffle >burp<!

Prime Minister …

Are you eating a baby?

Ah. Well. Umm. That is … *eughh!!* should have taken the nappy off first. Phwahhh!!

Blame for this unfortunate incident rests entirely with the baby, I'm afraid.

Infans culpam.

It showed no common sense in approaching the PM when he was hungry.

Scuffle!!

Stick him in the cupboard with Mark Francois, Liz Truss and all the other liabilities. I don't want to see any of them again till Xmas!

Now I need to speak to Mr Neil…

A senior Downing Street source has just told me that it was not Boris Johnson eating that baby; it was in fact Jeremy Corbyn in a cunning disguise. What a monster!!

Good thing we cleared that up. I'd hate to be spreading fake news!

BoJo's Woe Show

Edition 2

Crapping on Britain since August 2019

Catastrophus — *Copulatus*

9th November 2019

Tories caught selectively editing Labour videos. | **James Cleverly chickens out of an interview with Kay Burley.**

Hello I'm Kay Burley, and with me is Tory James Cleverly

Actually I have to go! I'm booked for a radio show

No you're not. We checked.

Oh. Errmm... Well I need to go to the toilet, then.

Sorry, you can't.

Why not?.

Because we glued your bottom to the chair.

Now, perhaps you can tell us why your party has been editing videos, to make voters think that Jeremy Corbyn is a Dalek?

Ummm … I ... I deny it!

Well let's watch the un-doctored video, shall we?

We will – let me explain – terminate all Tory tax cuts for the rich, while defending human rights and family life. This forms the core of our manifesto.

And now your party's doctored version …

We will … ex… terminate all … human … life … forms ...

W-we just trimmed it for length!

ex…terminate!

ex…terminate!

ex…terminate!

Helllp!!! Dominiiic!!

When will you release the Russia report?

Do all Tories think they're better than everyone else?

Boris is just a serial liar isn't he?

BoJo's Woe Show

Edition **3**

*Crapping on Britain
since August 2019*

11th November 2019

Catastrophus *Copulatus*

Johnson goes visiting hospitals

Kids locked in rooms as PM visits schools, so they can't ask questions

Phwaff! I'm here in a hospital! Great business opportunity!

What's that, Dom? Ah. Yes. Hospitals aren't for sale. Phwahh! Yes, ah ahh ahh not for sale, definitely not. No.

Now, let's meet some ordinary people. Seem to be thin on the ground today! Ah! There's one!

Privet, Tzar Boris. I vill be votink the Tory and all publik should be doing same or is very bad endink for your country.

Now here is many Rubles Vladimir said to be givink to you.

Not on camera, you idiot!!!

Phwaff! Looks like there's no-one else here to speak to. Phwahh!! On to the kittens' home, Dominic!

Mmf! Mmf!

Let us out!!

Unlock this door!

Shut up!

Bang Bang

We're doctors and we want our say!

BoJo's Woe Show

Edition 4

Crapping on Britain since August 2019

Catastrophus Copulatus

12th November 2019

BBC mysteriously uses older, more flattering footage of Johnson in place of current footage

Reports of secret deal between Tories and Nigel Farage

Bendy buses. Phwah!! Olympics. Feelgood factor! Bleh blehhh garden bridge fire brigade. Phwiff-phwaff! Bright future for London!!

The Prime Minister, giving his speech this morning. Diane Abbott, how will Labour respond to this?

Andrew, that wasn't this morning's speech. It's a recording of his London Mayor speech from 2014!

Now come on, Diane, the editor assures me …

I recorded his actual speech this morning! Look …

Phwaff! I'm going to get us a brilliant Brexit with my deal!

Now Boris, we agreed …

… a brilliant No-Deal Brexit. Yes. That's what I, ah ahh ahhh, meant. With Freedom of movement. I mean, no freedom of movement. Awful idea. Except in Northern Ireland because they get all the best bits. Phwoooff!! Or not. I've lost track of it a bit. Jeremy Corbyn smells!

Well they're barely different …

BoJo's Woe Show

Edition 5

Crapping on Britain since August 2019

Catastrophus Copulatus

14th November 2019

| **Yet another wave of destructive floods hits Britain** | **Tories promising inaction.** |

Our house is flooded! We've lost everything!

At least things can't get any worse.

Phwaff!!

Oh No!

We spoke too soon!

What-ho, you Northern plebians! Popped along to lend a hand. Any cameras about?

Get lost!

Are you going to find money to rebuild our house?

Good God, no! This is a Labour safe seat. Phwaff!! What do you think I am, an idiot?

Aha!! There's the camera crew! Quick, someone find me a mop!

Aaaaarrrggghhh!! Stop it! I'll give you a peerage!

MOP!

MOP!

BoJo's Woe Show

Edition **6**

*Crapping on Britain
since August 2019*

Catastrophus *Copulatus*

15th November 2019

**Half of Brexit Party candidates
suddenly stand down.**

**Massive boost to
Tories.**

I'm delighted to introduce Lord Cashface McBastard, our new Brexit Party candidate for Coalface North

Pssst!! McBastard!

Phwaff!! How about a double peerage, a knighthood and a million pounds, just to stand down and tell everyone that Farage is a wally! Phwoff!!

That's so unfair! I sold out 300 of my minions for you, and *this* is how you repay me??

Phwaff!! Now now, Nigel, don't be a ninny. You can have a peerage too!

I don't **want** a peerage!! I want to be **important**!

You were useful once, but now you're a bit in the way, old chum. So run along now. Phwaff!! I'm born to rule and you're not, you see. Just how it is.

Turncoat!!

BIFF!

BASH!

THUMP!

Irrelevance!!

Vote Tory for sound and trustworthy government

2 million, and you've got a deal

BoJo's Woe Show

Edition 7

Crapping on Britain since August 2019

18th November 2019

Catastrophus Copulatus

Dodgy dealings by Johnson with mistress Jennifer Arcuri	Prorogation of parliament confirmed as illegal.

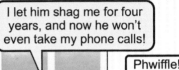
I let him shag me for four years, and now he won't even take my phone calls!

Phwiffle!

Prime Minister! Phone call for you

Oh, Phwattt!

I told you, get lost, you ugly fat cow! It's not my fault you were so gullible! Phwaff!! You were useful to me once, but now you're just soiled goods. So phwack off! Goodbye.

It's the Queen.

Ah.

I told you, *get lost* you senile old bint! It's not my fault you were so gullible! Phwaff!! You were useful to me once, but…

BoJo's Woe Show

Edition **8**

*Crapping on Britain
since August 2019*

Catastrophus   *Copulatus*

21st November 2019

Shock as Johnson actually turns up for leaders' debate

Tories caught pretending to be impartial fact checking source

---

They've cut the NHS so much it's at breaking point, and if they win, they'll sell it to the USA, and to big pharma

Prime Minister? Your response?

Hang on, I weh wehh wehhh … bleh! Have to nip for a pee!

This is a job for …

Fact Check Man!

Phwaff!! The real *impartial* truth is that we – I mean they, the Tories – have beh behh behhhh built 100 new hospitals *every month since 2010*! So there!!

Hang on … aren't you just Boris Johnson, with pants on your head?

Sehhhh sehh certainly not! Look, there's the real me over there! Phwaff!!

GET BREXIT DONE … Bzzz!
GET BREXIT DONE … Bzzz!
GET BREXIT DONE … Bzzz!

BoJo's Woe Show

Edition **9**

Crapping on Britain since August 2019

21st November 2019

Ordinary guy asks Johnson a killer question.

Confusion over why TV pundits can't do the same

Prime Minister, why won't you release the Russia Report?

Phwehh! Absolutely no evidence of Russian meddling! Phwaff! If there were, I'd have ah ahh ahhh seen it.

But Prime Minister, you lie all the time. I mean, literally, ALL the time. So forgive us if we don't believe you.

So we're going to keep asking, until you – mmmffff!!

Phwaff!!! Anyone else want to ask about the Russia Report? No?

GULAG TRANSPORT

Mmf! Mmf!

BoJo's Woe Show

Edition 10

Crapping on Britain since August 2019

Catastrophus *Copulatus*

22nd November 2019

"There's no magic money tree" – Theresa May

Tories promise lots of sudden spending if they win

Wehh wehh wehh right, chaps! We need a new source of money for after the election! Phwaff!!

For those promises you've been making? You mean we're actually going to **keep** some of them?

Dehhhh dehh deh don't be silly, Jeremy. It's to fund more tax cuts for billionaires. Vladimir insisted. Phwaff!!

We could pretend to ban fracking, then let the companies bribe us to bring it back?

Phwahh! We're already doing that. Gove? Any ideas?

Dancing pink seahorses and spinning turtles!!!

Oh phwack, he's been on the powder again. Patel?

It's simple. Let's tax people for being poor. They're a drain on resources. So the poorer they are, the more they pay. It's not our fault if the lazy gits can't be bothered finding rich parents

Genius, Patel!

Phwaff!! Top Plan!

Man!! The colours!

BoJo's Woe Show

Edition **11**

Crapping on Britain since August 2019

23rd November 2019

Catastrophus   Copulatus

| Johnson turns up to leaders' debate for 2nd time! | Audience member asks if he's a racist. |

BoJo's Woe Show

Edition 12

Crapping on Britain since August 2019

Catastrophus  *Copulatus*

23rd November 2019

Tories favoured by another BBC "production error"	Old lady in street delivers perfect description of Boris Johnson

Boris Johnson!

You're a disgrace to this country! The worst PM we've ever had, you filthy piece of toerag!! And what's more …

Oh shut up, you old harpy!!

BIFF!!

Boris you idiot! They're filming us!!

Lean over her, and pretend you care. I'll try to fix this!!

Later that day…

And here on the BBC, we can now show you exclusive footage …

… of the Prime Minister stopping to help an old lady who'd mysteriously collapsed in the street...

… edited for length, of course.

BoJo's Woe Show

Edition **13**

Crapping on Britain since August 2019

25th November 2019

Catastrophus *Copulatus*

Journalist asks Johnson a simple question

Johnson attempts to give a coherent answer, and fails.

So why did your HQ pretend to be an impartial fact checking site?

Ah. Well, uhhh, hmmm. Phwaff! Errr, don't really do twitter. Er, um, isn't Labour awful! um, er…

Facts!! There's one great big fact we have to hunt for, like the Snark, or … or Mogg's conscience, or Hunt's personality, or Gove's cocaine stash … or … or why Blake wasn't in the last 2 seasons of *Blakes* 7. Why was that? **Corbyn can't answer that!** Err, err…

Urgent note for you, PM!

Take the earpiece out of your NOSE, and put it in your EAR.
~ Dominic

Ah.

Phwaff!! Dominic! I can hear you now. What should I say?

What? … Ah! Got it.

Change the subject, you idiot!

Oh, you meant *me* change the subject … OK! Err … err … our plan is to … umm.. pretend there'll be 50000 new nurses! Is that right, Dom?

Hello, BBC? We're going to need your editing services again!

BoJo's Woe Show

Edition **14**

Crapping on Britain since August 2019

Catastrophus   *Copulatus*

26th November 2019

Not firing nurses is the same as hiring new ones, says Morgan

English language stretched to breaking point by Tory logic

Nicky Morgan, those 19000 'new' nurses are actually nurses that we already have, yes?

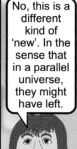

No, this is a different kind of 'new'. In the sense that in a parallel universe, they might have left.

Then they're not new, are they?

I've got a dictionary here, if you don't know what "new" means.

Well we'll *make* them new, by firing them all, then rehiring them on worse contracts!

That still means there won't be any more nurses than we had before!

Yes there will! You see, we *could* have fired them then not re-hired them!

Let's try again. If you got fired, then someone rehired you the next day

Though God knows why

… there'd STILL only be *one* Nicky Morgan in government

Thankfully.

No you're wrong! Look, see, I'm Nicky Morgan …

and I'm Nicky Gorgan, too!

Vote Tory for a getter Gritain!

Morgan! You're fired for total incompetence!

But Sock Boy here shows promise. Want to be Foreign Secretary?

Yes glease!

BoJo's Woe Show

Edition 15

Crapping on Britain since August 2019

26th November 2019

Catastrophus *Copulatus*

Chief Rabbi endorses the Tories	**Archbishop of Canterbury comes out for Johnson, too.**

Jeremy Corbyn has been a bit rubbish at handling antisemitism, so you'd better vote for the outright racists in the Tory party instead.

Verily, he doth speak the truth! Vote Tory, for it is given to all that men who went to Eton are anointed by God to rule over us, and thereby to shower the world's riches upon the already fortunate, while the meek must increase their Godly suffering.

Food banks! Universal Credit! No Deal Brexit! Climate Denial! Shameless lying!! Xenophobia! Promoting violence and bullying! Priti Patel!!! This Boris Johnson is my kinda guy!! Vote Tory to make Britain Hell on Earth! Go, Boris, go, Boris, Go! Go!! Go!!!

Phwaffle!!! Ah, yes, Thank you, yes. I'll build you 19000 new synagogues, churches, and … public schools. Out of existing ones. Phwaff!! No offence, but I think we might ask the BBC to edit one of them out? Protect the brand, you know. I mean, is *anyone* a Christian anymore?

BoJo's Woe Show

Edition 16

Crapping on Britain since August 2019

Catastrophus *Copulatus*

27th November 2019

| Stormzy makes a political comment | Gove provides David Brent level cringeworthy response |

Michael Gove, you baselessly accused Stormzy of knowing nothing about politics, and then made a risible attempt to sound cool on Twitter. You've made a bit of an idiot of yourself, haven't you?

I set duh trends dat dem man follow
Mah bitch don't spit, she always swallow
I ride da streets of London – Nice!
While mah chauffer plays Vanilla Ice

Gimme some beats, DJ Moggsy!
I'm MC Gove, an' I'm just cool!
I cut da fundin' to yo school!

We – we – we – we – w we - we – we – we're all going on a sum – su – sum – sum mmer hel ho – hol hol – – ho – h ol –((fo holiday no – – no – – no – no no – no more wo wo – – wo

Mr Gove, please stop!!!

I've never seen anything so painfully embarrassing *in all my life!!* And I've sat next to Piers Morgan every morning for the last 4 years.

Think I'm not hip? Then watch this!!

SNORRRT!

See? All the sparkling blue lobsters and glowfish agree with me!

BoJo's Woe Show

Edition **16**

Crapping on Britain since August 2019

Catastrophus   Copulatus

27th November 2019

"The NHS is about as safe with them as a pet hamster would be with a hungry python." John Major.

Thehhh theh the NHS is not for sale! Phwaff!! Certainly not. Errrmm… no.

NHS Hospital

I promise I won't sell it unless Donald asks *really* nicely. And even then, I won't! Phwaff!

Whatever Corbyn says, whatever the civil service or the doctors or the evidence says, it's not for sale. Completely safe with me.

SHIP TO USA

Not selling, ah ahh ahhhh absolutely not. I'll be found dead in a ditch before that happens. Even more dead than last time! Phwaff!!

SOLD

PROPERTY OF D. TRUMP

Oy! Scarecrow! Get lost! New owner wants you out the building!

You see? Perfectly safe! Phwaff!

We're losing the patient!

Fetch the leeches!

NHS Hospital

BoJo's Woe Show

Edition **18**

*Crapping on Britain
since August 2019*

Catastrophus   *Copulatus*

28th November 2019

| Johnson can't be bothered attending debate about climate change | But his dad turns up, late, with Gove. |

So let's hear what the party leaders have to say on climate change ...

It is the single most important issue that we face, and we need to act urgently.

The beardie scruff is right, for once! We have to work together on this issue

I agree.

Well said

This goes far beyond party politics.

Well, Boris Johnson couldn't be here due to a prior engagement with one of his families. But we've got this from the BBC …

Well, this is ahhhh vehhh veh very important subject. Very important! Phwaff!! There are of course strong arguments on both sides, yes, bahhhh bah but on the whole I'd have to say …

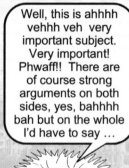

… that putting tea in the cup *before* milk is better, Laura. Phwaff!

Thank you for that wonderful insight, you rugged hunk, you! Now, what else would you like to be asked about?

BoJo's Woe Show

Edition **19**

Crapping on Britain since August 2019

Catastrophus Copulatus

29th November 2019

Another tower block burns after Grenfell lessons were ignored.

Johnson starts to establish his "friendly interviewers only" pattern

Tonight on Channel 4 news, yet another building is on fire with flammable cladding, and the fire brigade have too few engines to deal with it, after 9 years of cuts!

Cripes! This is an emergency! I'd better get my best team out there, straight away! Phwaff!!

Pwiffity-phwaffity! My boy Boris wanted to have a lot more firemen and get rid of cladding, but that nasty Nicola Sturgeon wouldn't let him. Phwoof!

Pretty reds and yellows

We've just heard that Michael Gove has offered to put out the fire with his army of diamond-breathing unicorns. His offer has understandably been declined.

Oh. That's the phone.

BRRRING!

Is that Channel 4? This is your last warning!! Either you report things *my* way, or you get a visit from Vlad's boys. Capische?

BoJo's Woe Show

Edition **20**

*Crapping on Britain
since August 2019*

Catastrophus  *Copulatus*

29th November 2019

**Johnson promises to be
a fearless negotiator of
trade deals.**

**Corbyn was grilled by Andrew Neil,
but Johnson dodged out of this.**

Wehh weh wehhh once we get Brexit done, I'll be getting a brilliant trade deal with the EU, and with America, and every other country. All by next Xmas!! Phwaff!!

We shall be fearless!! Phwaff!! Donald Trump may be the world's most powerful man, but I shall stehhh steh stehh stand tall for Britain! Nothing will intimidate me!

DING-DONG!

Go find out who that is, Perkins!

Yes, PM.

Is Boris in? I'd like to speak to him.

Ummm … I'll check, Mr Neil.

Has he gone yet has he gone yet has he gone yet????

BoJo's Woe Show

Edition 21

Crapping on Britain since August 2019

Catastrophus  *Copulatus*

1st December 2019

Election campaign suspended after Terrorist attack on London Bridge

Supposedly.

The main message we all have to take home from this week's tragedy in London …

… is that everything that has gone wrong in the last 9 years is Labour's fault!!

They made us cut 20000 police officers! And then the bastards distracted us with Brexit for four years!!

So while election campaigning is suspended, what other free political points would you like to score?

Nehh neh nehhh new policies! Tough on crime, tough on terror! Phwaff!! Lots of things we forgot to do since 2010, because of Labour, that we're absolutely definitely going to do now. Gehhh geh gehh get Brexit done. Phwaff!!

PM! Red alert!

You need to clear the building, now!!

Terrorist!?

Worse!! I've just seen Andrew Neil!

Save me!!!

BoJo's Woe Show

Edition **22**

Crapping on Britain since August 2019

2nd December 2019

Catastrophus  *Copulatus*

Johnson skips out of two TV leaders' debates.	Rishi Sunak (who's he??) takes his place.

Blah blah … bright future … drone drone … great plans … blah blah … get Brexit done …

Mr Sunak?

Hmm?

This is all very well, but you haven't actually told us which child you are here for.

Ummm … actually, Boris forgot to tell me. I'm waiting for him to call me back.

I wouldn't bother. He doesn't remember her name, either. Or her half-brother's.

You do know this is meant to be a parents' evening, not a parents' substitutes evening?

Shut up or we'll have Ofsted close you down.

BRRRING!

Ah, that'll be Boris.

Hello PM … what? 11 am tomorrow at your alimony hearing? Yes I can do that

… paternity test at 2pm? Well I could go along but they might notice the difference …

… and could you pop along to Uxbridge for me on Election Night? I'd sooner skip the count just in case I get Portilloed!

Plus I've no idea where Uxbridge is.

BoJo's Woe Show

Edition **23**

Crapping on Britain since August 2019

2nd December 2019

Catastrophus Copulatus

"Sequence the DNA of all new babies" says Matt Hancock | The idea is soon quietly dropped

So I've got this great new plan – full genetic sequencing of every new baby born in Britain!

Brilliant plan, Hancock!! We can screen them for genetic evidence of leftiness or excessive compassion! And have problem babies humanely destroyed.

Or sent abroad to work as chimney sweeps

Hancock you moron!!!!

You need to dehhh deh dehhh drop this plan immediately!!! Have you **any idea** how much it will cost? Phwaff!!!

I-i-it won't cost us anything, PM! We're going to make the plebs pay for it!

Not the country, you stupid idiot! **ME**! All my bloody ex-fillies will use the data to prove I'm the dad!! It'll bankrupt me!

BoJo's Woe Show

Edition 24

Crapping on Britain since August 2019

3rd December 2019

Catastrophus Copulatus

Trump decides to visit Britain

Just days before the election

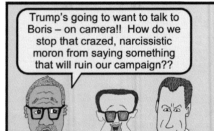

Trump's going to want to talk to Boris – on camera!! How do we stop that crazed, narcissistic moron from saying something that will ruin our campaign??

Just let me stand in for him again!

He meant Trump, Sunak, you idiot! Still, it gives me an idea …

Welcome to Britain, Mr Trump. The Queen has laid on a three day orgy of pussy-grabbing for you in a remote Scottish castle

Those lucky girls! I'm so great!

Woof! woof! can I go too?

We now go live to the joint press conference with our PM, and the President.

The NHS is safe … great trade deal … the NHS is safe …

Get Brexit done … get Brexit done … get Brexit done …

Meanwhile in Scotland

Phwaff! Ow!! Stop scratching me!

Where are all the girls??

Meow!

Wraaow!!

BoJo's Woe Show

Edition **25**

*Crapping on Britain
since August 2019*

Catastrophus   *Copulatus*

4th December 2019

Celebrities line up to endorse Labour

One British Royal has become *persona non grata*

Our poll lead is slipping! We might need to change strategy … and actually *do* something!

I kehh kehh can't hide any more than I already am! Phwaff!

How about Compulsory rectal examinations for all women under 30?

Close all the food banks so the scroungers are too hungry to vote.

I can see dragons

Require every voter to present his butler when voting. *Nil suffragato sine butlerum*

What's really killing us is celebrity endorsements. Hugh Grant's been helping the lefties with his bumbling posh charm!

But *I've* got that! Phwaff!

Yes but he's only a bastard in **films**. And there's lots more celebs backing them, too!

The only endorsements *we've* got are extreme far right: Trump, Tommy Robinson and Julia Hartley-Brewer!

Well if we can't get any celebs to back us … I've got an idea. Hancock, do exactly as I say …

Yes, happy to publicly endorse you, old chap. Bit of a loose end just now, you know. Which party are you?

Labour. I'm Jeremy Corbyn. Thanks, Prince Andrew!

BoJo's Woe Show

Edition **26**

Crapping on Britain since August 2019

5th December 2019

Catastrophus

Copulatus

"I've never met him, and I don't know who he is" says Trump of Prince Andrew.

Corbyn under fire for not watching Queen's speech.

Donald Trump says he's never met Prince Andrew, despite playing golf with him months earlier. Is he senile, or a liar?

Ah, wehhhh weh wehh well, you see. Hmmm. Very good question. Errrr …. Get Brexit done. That's what matters, eh? Phwaff!! Err… errrm … do feel free to interrupt … um

… Jeremy Corbyn!! Let's talk about him instead. He doesn't watch the Queen's at Xmas, you know. What a traitor!! Phwaff!! I watch it. In fact I watch recordings of it *every single morning* over breakfast, so there!!

Really? So what did she say, in the most recent one?

Ehhhhrrr. Ah, well, errr... umm... Hmm. Very good question. Ummm …. She talks about Queeny things. Yes. And Queening. And family, but probably not Prince Andrew. Phwaff!! Next question!

Some people say you're becoming increasingly like Donald Trump, Prime Minister. So I ask again, do you think he's senile, or a serial liar, or both?

Trump? I've never met him, and I don't know who he is!!

BoJo's Woe Show

Crapping on Britain since August 2019

Catastrophus Copulatus

Special Archive Edition

EXCLUSIVE: Footage uncovered of Johnson, David Davis and Michael Gove as schoolchildren

Footage might offer insights into Brexitty mindset, claim psychologists

BoJo's Woe Show

Edition **28**

Crapping on Britain since August 2019

11th December 2019

Catastrophus Copulatus

Tories still ahead in the polls with 3 days to go

Psychologists confess they are unable to explain it.

I'll be voting Tory. They're the only ones who can fix everything that's gone wrong with Britain in the last nine years.

I lost my job and my house last year, but thanks to the Tories I've still got my lovely wife, and my nice red car.

Three of my mates sleep rough now, but we're in a lovely hostel room with a shared bathroom

SMASH!!

I'm sure they'll restore my benefit payments next year. It's fair enough that they got accidentally stopped, 'cos there's a lot of crooks and scroungers out there.

MUG 100 PC

I trust Boris and the Tories completely!

BoJo's Woe Show

Edition **29**

Crapping on Britain since August 2019

9th December 2019

Catastrophus Copulatus

Johnson snatches phone, to avoid questions about dire state of NHS

Tories try to claim assault following an obvious accident

Prime Minister! Here's a picture of a child with pneumonia, sleeping on a hospital floor! What will you do about it?

Give me that!!!

SNATCH

Look at the picture, Mr Johnson!

What picture? Now get lost, I'm busy.

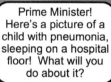

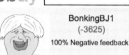

Mr Johnson, is it true that you are an utterly heartless bastard, with less compassion and humanity than a Dalek?

Oh shut up!

BIFF!!!

I think this woman needs an ambulance.

What woman? I can't see her.

Hello? Ms Kuenssberg? A leftie just punched Boris in the fist with her nose!

BoJo's Woe Show

Edition **30**

Crapping on Britain since August 2019

10th December 2019

Catastrophus 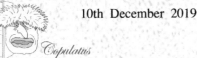 *Copulatus*

Dr Rosena Allin-Khan creates a lovely, clever election ad based on *Love Actually*. | **The Tories shamelessly copy it, and many are taken in by it.**

I wish they'd just *get Brexit done*.

Yes, I did not approve of all that *parliamentary scrutiny* that MPs insisted upon.

Try to sound natural, you idiots!

Brrrinng!!!

I'll get it

Pretend it's carol singers

Er, why? My husband's a Tory, too.

I don't bloody know. I just do what Dominic tells me to.

We nicked this idea from Labour.

Here are ten reasons to vote for me.
1. Get Brexit done.

2. Errrmmm ...

ummm ... ummm ... errr ... hmmm ...

Can we skip to the bit of the film where the PM runs off with the sexy young waitress?

Who is it, mummy?

Uh-oh.

Oh phwack! Is he one of mine?? You do look vaguely familiar.

Who is it, mum?

It's ... oh, he's run away.

Hey! He's nicked my phone!

BoJo's Woe Show

Edition **31**

Crapping on Britain
since August 2019

11th December 2019

Catastrophus Copulatus

Johnson pretends to deliver milk in another staged election stunt.

PM hides in fridge to avoid questions from GMTV

Hello, you sexy filly! I've come to put some **milky goodness** into you. Phwaff!

So, are you looking forward to a **good, hard Brexit**?

Absolutely not!! Brexit is an utterly stupid idea, and it always has been!!

Oh. Ahhh … ahh … um… errr …

I don't believe it! The fat ape's gone to the *wrong house*!! **Stop filming!!**

Well if we're not making a film, perhaps we can make some babies instead! I'm good at that!

Get rid of him get rid of him!

Er … you can stay if you want, but I've got Piers Morgan and Andrew Neil coming by soon

EEK!!

Phwack! Phwacketty - Phwack!! Why's there never enough room in these things?

BoJo's Woe Show

Edition **32**

Crapping on Britain since August 2019

13th December 2019

Catastrophus *Copulatus*

Johnson's Tories win the election. No I don't know how, either.

PM offers empty promises of reconciliation

I want to behh beh behhh bring the country together with some sexual healing … I mean healing. Phwaff!!

So will you apologise for all the horrible things you've said about Muslims?

Who said that? I don't see anyone. That reminds me, I need to post a letter.

Aaaaarggghhh!!

You've made my wife and 3 million others feel unsafe and unwelcome here! What will you do about that?

Woof!!! What a filly! Let me borrow her for a night, and I'll see if she merits some **special treatment** …

You're not interested in reconciling people at all, are you, you bastard!

I am! And you can all start by apologising to my friends here for calling them gammons and racists!

OUT FORRIN

ALL THE UZLIMS

BRITTIN FIRST

BoJo's Woe Show

Edition **33**

Crapping on Britain since August 2019

Catastrophus Copulatus

14th December 2019

Right wingers are becoming increasingly obsessed with winning for its own sake.

While some on the left seem to have the exact opposite problem.

BoJo's Woe Show

Edition **34**

Crapping on Britain since August 2019

16th December 2019

Catastrophus *Copulatus*

Beliefs and desires are not the same thing as facts, no matter who you are.	Irish border issue remains unsolved.

OK, PM, we can't put it off any longer. Will it be a border down the Irish Sea, a land border between NI and Ireland, or all of us staying in the Customs Union?

Ah, behhh beh behh but no but not an issue. Phwaff!!

We won the election, so now we can Get Brexit Done, and that means no Customs Union, and no Borders anywhere!

No, no, we have to do one of those three things. It's unavoidable

Spirals of silkworm pearls

But I *said* we won't do any of it, and I won! So that's the final word!! Phwaff!!

Sorry, PM, but I think you need to look at Mogg's Venn diagram again

What we told the voters

What's actually true

BoJo's Woe Show

Edition **35**

Crapping on Britain since August 2019

17th December 2019

Catastrophus *Copulatus*

Nicky Morgan decides not to stand again during 2019 election

But she gets a cabinet job anyway

So we'll make Nicky Morgan culture secretary, even though she stood down, and so no-one voted for her.

No-one? I thought I got 50,000 new votes, including existing ones.

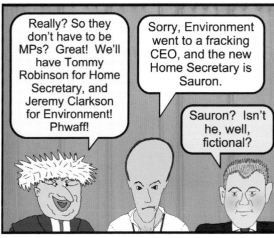

Really? So they don't have to be MPs? Great! We'll have Tommy Robinson for Home Secretary, and Jeremy Clarkson for Environment! Phwaff!

Sorry, Environment went to a fracking CEO, and the new Home Secretary is Sauron.

Sauron? Isn't he, well, fictional?

Yes, but we'll just stick a giant eye on top of Big Ben. Rees Mogg will give the actual orders. No-one will know the difference.

What about me, you useless half-wits?

*If Ex-MPs can be in charge, then so can **dead PMs**! So move aside, you hapless muppets, and kneel before the ghost of Maggie!!*

EEEK!!

I think I've wet my pants.

BoJo's Woe Show

Edition **36**

*Crapping on Britain
since August 2019*

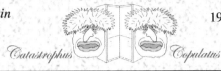

Catastrophus   Copulatus

19th December 2019

Tory mental gymnastics over numbers of "new" nurses continues

Countdown star celebrates Tory win on Twitter

We'll make 50000 nurses … out of existing nurses … by cloning or something

If you start with 50000 and you don't take away the 19000 that aren't actually new, then you still have 50000.

You're both *phwacking useless*! I need a Tory who can actually do maths …

Get me **Rachel Riley**!

Well Boris, if you add 13K to 18K, and then do a lot of bullshitting, I calculate that there's f**k all the voters can do about it, now the election is over.

Baroness Riley, you're my new Health Secretary. Hancock, you're fired!

What?? But what'll I do, now?

I know where there'll be a vacancy…

Matt Hancock, the target was 150. Could it be done?

I think this one was impossible, Nick.

150

25 100 50 10 5 3

Xmas Eve, 2021.

There's NO ROOM for you here. Can't you read? Boris won, so you can piss off back to your own country.

Gammonview Inn

NO Jews, Muslims, Corrins or Darkies

But I'm carrying the Son of God! The Second Coming!

No yer not. Jesus wuz **English**!! So get lost!

We'll have to go to a hospital!

We can't! They're not allowed to admit us now, without proof of UK citizenship.

Let's find an empty barn. There's lots since all the farms went bust.

Uhhhhh … aaaagghhh …. It's coming!!

Sorry, no wise men. They couldn't get visas.

Keep pushing! I can see the head!!

Waaahhh!!

Vote Bernard Matthews to Get Xmas Done!

Wait a minute!! That's not the Son of God! More like the son of … **Boris Johnson**!!

I'm sorry!! He got me drunk!

Phwaffle!

BoJo's Woe Show

Edition **38**

Crapping on Britain since August 2019

Catastrophus   Copulatus

28th December 2019

Johnson goes on holiday in Caribbean	"I'll be found dead in a ditch" before I delay Brexit, PM says	*Death in Paradise* returns for new series

So who's the corpse this week then Ted … I mean, Dwayne?

Some fat blond British bloke. Been dead since October!

Is it 4 suspects this week, or 5?

Uhh, 66 million, Chief. Plus another 50 wronged husbands.

Ahh, feck. This could take more than 60 minutes to solve!

I don't think we've even got that long, Chief! I've heard there's a voodoo necromancer in town!!

Brexittieau zombificae Putino mondae merdieau!

Ge-e-e-t brrrexiiiiit dooooonnnnne …

Aaiieeee!! We're all doomed!!

BoJo's Woe Show

Edition **39**

Crapping on Britain since August 2019

4th January 2019

Catastrophus ... *Copulatus*

Australia is on fire	Trump assassinates Iranian general	Johnson is still on holiday

THE MURDOCH TIMES

Edition **40**

5th January 2020

We Obey No-One. We Are The Super-Rich. Obey Us! Obeyyyyyyy!!!

Australia fires "caused by leftie arsonsts" says non-expert.

Greta Thunberg should shut up, says renowned climate expert Meatloaf.

OUR CLIMATE CHANGE DENIAL PLAN SUCCEEEDS. AUSTRALIA IS BURNING!

Exssselent!!

BUT THOSE WORLD LEADERS NOT UNDER OUR CONTROL ARE EXPRESSING CONCERN!

Distract them. Tell useful idiot Trump that someone in Iran said something mean about him on Twitter

IRAN WAR PLAN SUCCESSFUL! BUT FIRES IN AUSTRALIA NOW CAUSING PUBLIC CONCERN!

Tell them it's all just caused by a few arsonists, and not enough fire-breaks.

THAT IS AB-SURRRD! NO HUMAN WILL ACCEPT IT!

But they will!!! I have taught them to believe!!

WHAT ABOUT THE THUNBERG FEMALE? WE HAVE NOT BEEN ABLE TO SILENCE HER!

Hack her phone. Then find some ageing, has-been pop star, and feed him up our "she's been brain-washed" story!

BoJo's Woe Show

Edition **41**

*Crapping on Britain
since August 2019*

Catastrophus *Copulatus*

7th January 2019

Johnson proposes "Festival of Brexit" to rub salt in Remainer wounds

Cummings shows off builder chic

Phwaff! I've decided to spaff away billions on a festival of Brex … I mean, Britain!!

I *suppose* I'll allow it. But *I* choose the staff

THE BOSS

… so that's the brief. Anything that annoys lefties, Remoaners or the PC lot.

Yeah! Bladdy snowflakes need ta get a sense uv *humour*!

Let's all black up, and burn some EU flags!

Wot about for Muslims?

Let's make big, big posters of sausages, bacon and ... what else is from pigs??

Gammon.

Hey! You can't call us that!

That's *racist*, that is!

I'm calling the **police** on you!

BoJo's Woe Show

Edition **42**

*Crapping on Britain
since August 2019*

9th January 2019

Catastrophus *Copulatus*

"I'm a Tory, but I'm OK", writes new MP Virginia Crosbie in *The Times*.

Dubs amendment voted down by Tories

Hello! I'm one of the new intake of Tory MPs. But please don't judge me by my party. I'm actually a really nice person.

I'm here to make a difference for ordinary people.

Vote on Amendment to give EU citizens who live here the right of appeal against deportation. DIVISION!

Oooh! Excuse me! This is exciting, isn't it?

Family, justice, fairness, honesty. These things matter to me.

NO   AYE

Vote on Amendment to protect the rights of child refugees. DIVISION!

I'm a mum, you know. My kids mean the world to me.

NO   AYE

BoJo's Woe Show

Edition **43**

Crapping on Britain since August 2019

11th January 2019

Catastrophus Copulatus

Meghan and Harry quit Britain!!

Well PM, it seems we're down one prince and princess!

I can't think *what* made them want to leave!

Exeunt, pursued a tabloidum

You don't think it could have been … the press, do you?

Daily Extreme

GRETA THUNBERG **MURDERED**
PRINCESS DIANA – NEW EVIDENCE!!

Meghan Markle? What a total, utter c**t! She should f**k off back to Bongo-Bongo land.

Daily Mail

VOTING LABOUR GIVES YOU CANCER, SAYS TOP BLOGGER

Monstrous, Evil Black Witch steals Harry away from tearful Queen.

No, Mr Hunt, it could not. Understand me?

Y-yes Mr Murdoch, sorry Mr Murdoch sir.

I … guess we just have to be nicer to people if we want them to stick around.

Phwaff! Anyway, on to NHS understaffing. It's all the fault of those smelly foreign nurses, who are leaving in droves. How do we persuade those awful, queue-jumping squatters to stay here?

BoJo's Woe Show

Edition **44**

Crapping on Britain since August 2019

13th January 2019

Catastrophus *Copulatus*

Johnson decides to ban use of the word "Brexit"

Yes, because it's the word that's going to cause all the damage.

That's it all set up, Guv.

Right, listen, you lot! From now on, if ANY member of my cabinet mentions thehhhh theh thehhh THAT word, a trapdoor will open, and dump you into a cesspit! Phwaff!!

Which word, Boz? 'Macbeth'?

'Jehovah'?

No you fools! I mean the B-word!!

What, 'Bendy Bananas'?

Beautiful Blue Buttercups

Bogies?

For goodness' sake you morons! BREXIT!! No-one's allowed to say –

Aaaaaarrgh!!

BoJo's Woe Show

Edition **45**

Crapping on Britain since August 2019

Catastrophus — *Copulatus*

14th January 2019

The Russia report, examining meddling in UK democracy, was ready for release before the 2019 election. They sat on it.

Where's the Russia Report? You said we'd see it after the election.

And you *believed* us?!?! Well we can't release it just now because … let me think … I know! We need a new select committee chair.

Brandon Lewis, it's now summer. where's the Russia Report?

Well I'm going to keep asking.

Sorry, we're all going on holiday for 4 months, now.

We can't release it this year, we're busy rigging – I mean preparing for – the 2024 election.

A dog ate my copy, on the way to the studio.

I'm afraid we left the last remaining copy in Norwich, which as you know Andrew has been underwater since 2042.

BoJo's Woe Show

Edition **46**

Crapping on Britain since August 2019

Catastrophus   Copulatus

14th January 2019

"Bung a bob for BigBenBong" launched

Scheme encourages ordinary Brits to make themselves poorer, in exchange for a pointless and divisive symbolic gesture. Like Brexit.

Phwoffle!! Big Ben *will* bong for Brexit! But only if the plebs pay for it! Phwaff!!

Wow! I'm in! I'll donate 50 pounds!!

I can't think of a more worthy cause, to spend my redundancy money on!

Spare us 10p, guv? I 'aven't eaten since yesterday, and me wee doggie is starvin'

Get lost.

At last, we have a government that thinks about the little guy, and what really matters.

NHS Medical Practice

Closed due to funding cuts

Nigel! You'll be donating to the Big Ben fund, won't you?

Sorry, I can't. I've only got £153,000 to last me till my next *Question Time* appearance.

Next week.

...due to ...ding cuts

BoJo's Woe Show

Edition **47**

*Crapping on Britain
since August 2019*

Catastrophus   *Copulatus*

15th January 2019

Johnson makes another attempt to sound statesmanlike, and fails.	**Priti Patel decides to classify Extinction Rebellion as terrorists.**

I can fehh feh feel the hand of history. Yes!!! The **hand of history** upon my shoulder. Phwaff!!

Tap! Tap!

Officer it wasn't me!! They *made* me take the money!! The kid's not mine you can't prove it!

The postal votes were Raab's idea!!!

Patel!!! You almost gave me a heart attack!!

Honestly Boz, I keep telling you, I've shut down all the police investigations. You need to stop being so jumpy, and –

Aaaiiieeeee!!! Terrorisssst!!!! Ruuuuunnnnn!

Evacuate the building! Call a SWAT team!! Get a narwhal tusk!! Save meeeeeeee!!!

BoJo's Woe Show

Edition **48**

Crapping on Britain since August 2019

17th January 2019

Catastrophus   Copulatus

Extremists of all kinds have a long history of radicalizing the emotionally vulnerable.	Celebrities who've had serious mental breakdowns may be especially susceptible.

QUESTION TIME …

Laurence Fox?

There's no such thing as racism … except against white people.

I mean … next you'll be saying there are people in this country who *didn't* grow up in mansions with rich and famous dads. It's f**king leftie nonsense.

Am on I fire, by the way? Do I look on fire? No? Then neither is Australia. Bloody lefties are making that up, just like they made up racism, climate change and the Holocaust, all to spoil MY life.

Good news, Bodge! I think we've found an actor to star in that film series you're planning!

But we don't have a script yet! Phwaff!!

Don't think you're gonna need one.

My wife is Billie Piper.

BoJo's Woe Show

Edition **49**

*Crapping on Britain
since August 2019*

22nd January 2019

Catastrophus Copulatus

Lie detectors are known to be untrustworthy and ineffective.	Like attracts like, so they say …

BoJo's Woe Show

Edition 50

Crapping on Britain since August 2019

Catastrophus Copulatus

23rd January 2019

Johnson invites people to submit their own questions to him for "Peoples' PMQs"

Of course, he only chooses the friendliest ones to answer.

I know! I'll ah ahh ahhh answer some questions from the public! Phwaff!

Uhhh, not sure that's a good idea, Bozz.

Nonsense! They all love me! Phwaff!

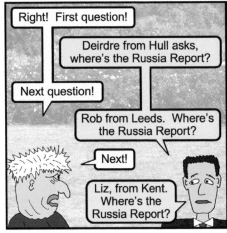

Right! First question!

Deirdre from Hull asks, where's the Russia Report?

Next question!

Rob from Leeds. Where's the Russia Report?

Next!

Liz, from Kent. Where's the Russia Report?

Angus from from Ballachulish. Where's the Russia Report?

Bahhh! How many more like that?

473. Plus another 50 "how many kids have you got?"

For goodness' sake, give me your phone …

THE BOSS

New call! Dom from London asks, what shampoo do you use?

At last, a proper question! Quick! Roll cameras!!

BoJo's Woe Show

Edition **51**

Crapping on Britain since August 2019

24th January 2019

Catastrophus  *Copulatus*

Archbishop of Canterbury re-states his views, and wonders why church is losing relevance	**Dubs amendment, protecting refugee children, falls.**

It's a disgrace! Totally immoral!!

I know, Archbishop. Those poor kids!

Daily Mail

THE FILM '*GHANDI*' HAD TOO MANY BROWN PEOPLE SAYS LAURENCE FOX

NO protection for refugee children. Dubs amendment rejected by MPs

Will of the People! We don't care about you, we're staying that way...

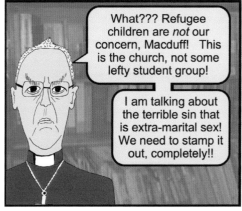

What??? Refugee children are *not* our concern, Macduff! This is the church, not some lefty student group!

I am talking about the terrible sin that is extra-marital sex! We need to stamp it out, completely!!

You should probably start with the Prime Minister.

He's exempt. He and I have made a deal …

In breaking news, Parliament has just passed a new law …

To celebrate our triumph over the EU, from next month all households must by law display a huge picture of Boris Johnson in every bedroom.

Yep! That should kill off sex, entirely!!

BoJo's Woe Show

Edition **52**

Crapping on Britain since August 2019

Catastrophus  *Copulatus*

1st February 2019

Britain has left the EU.	**Remainers mourn.**	**Brexitters are still just as angry as they always are.**

I did it Phwaff! **I got Brexit done!** *I am better than Churchill, I am better than Churchill, na-na-na-na! Hey!*

Well done, Boss!

Thank you. But now the real hard work begins.

Wh-what? **Dom!** You never said anything to me about having to **work!!**

Well there's border arrangements, trade deals to do …

New Jam Markets!!

Don't be absurd, Sunak. I'm talking about all the donors we need to start paying back, using public money.

But don't worry, you useless fat lump of horse dung, this is a job for **capable** people.

So I've booked you 11 months' holiday, somewhere no-one will find you

Then when No Deal's assured, we can both run off to the Cayman Isles.

But what happens if there's a major national or global crisis later in the year?

THE SUNDAY TIMES
Fears over deadly new virus in China

Well of course it wouldn't do to have a total vacuum of leadership at No. 10, during a time of major crisis.

So we'd have to keep Boris **completely** out of the way until the crisis had passed

THE BOSS

Misjudgement Day is coming!!!

"FOUL, WORTHLESS CREATURES!!!! WHY HAVE YOU VIOLATED MY CHAMBERS?" Flames roared around the huge body of Satan Beelzebub III as he spoke.

"I-i-i-it's an emergency Cabal m-m-meeting, my Lord," said Horsley. Like everyone in the room, he was bright red and possessed of horns and a tail. They ranged from four to eight feet tall, and Horsley was the smallest, and hence the most junior.

"He knows that, you useless idiot!" snapped Aldershot, smacking the back of Horsley's head with his tail. "That's his traditional greeting. Now tell him what you found. Now!!"

"M-m-m-me?"

"Yes, Horsley, you!" yelled Aldershot. He was tall and thin with a cropped moustache, and was standing bolt upright. "Sit up straight, you useless cassock," he added. "You're a disgrace!"

The terrified junior Devil tried for a moment to compose himself. "We found Fenwick, sir!" he blurted. "In Room Zero!"

"Found?" said Satan, cocking his head to the side. "I wasn't aware he'd been mislaid. What was he doing in there?"

"H-h-he was lying on the floor going 'mmm-mmm-mmm'," said Horsley.

"You mean he was bound and gagged?" asked Woking, the Ruler of English Hell. Other than the eight-foot Satan, he was the largest and most senior Devil in the room. He had a broad face with a triangular beard that reached his ears, and an even broader belly.

"Y-y-yes, sir," said Horsley. "The human souls appear to … errr … they've been using him as furniture, sirs!"

"Furniture?" asked Woking.

"Futons, mainly," quivered Horsley.

"Thank Lucifer we found out quickly," said Woking, stroking his red beard.

"If you call 23 years 'quickly', then yes, thank Lucifer," said Horsley.

"Twenty-three YEARS??" boomed Satan. "Aldershot?! You have mislaid an underling for more than two decades!? Explain!!"

Aldershot's mouth hung open, his pointed teeth glinting in the firelight. "Fenwick is a proven incompetent – Sir!" he proclaimed. "Not fit for service – Sir!"

"And you did NOTHING? All this time??" roared the Lord of Hell.

"We assumed he'd got lost – Sir!" barked Aldershot. "For the ongoing glory of Hell, a year without Fenwick is a year without reportable incidents – Sir! Hell is better off without him – Sir!"

"But it WAS a reportable incident," countered Woking.

"He was being used as furniture!" roared Satan. "By condemned souls who should have had none. For twenty-three YEARS!!"

"L-like I said, incompetent!" said Aldershot. "Sir!" he added quickly. He remained rigidly upright, but his tail was swishing around behind him like that of a frustrated cat.

"Gabriel's wings!!" bellowed Satan. "What a disaster!"

The others all winced.

"What does Fenwick have to say about this?" asked Woking.

"Nothing so far, sir" said Camberley.

"Why not?" demanded Woking.

"Because no-one has untied him yet."

"Mmm-hmm-bbllhh-hhmmbllhhhm--hmmmphhh!" said a voice from the far corner of the room.

Book 2 is coming!
Book 3 will follow!
(and book 4, if he lasts long enough)

BoJo's

World-beating!

Woe Show

Coming soon

CLOSED DUE TO INCOMPETENT PANDEMIC MISMANAGEMENT

Book 2: "A plague of idiots"

For your regular, up to date dose of abject Johnsonian Woe, follow @milneorchid on Twitter! (or watch the TV news)

Printed in Great Britain
by Amazon